FASHION
ACADEMY

Designer Drama

Also by Sheryl Berk and Carrie Berk

FASHION
ACADEMY

*Designer
Drama*

Sheryl Berk & Carrie Berk

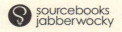
sourcebooks
jabberwocky

Published by Sourcebooks Jabberwocky, an imprint of Sourcebooks, Inc.
P.O. Box 4410, Naperville, Illinois 60567-4410
(630) 961-3900
Fax: (630) 961-2168
www.sourcebooks.com

Library of Congress Cataloging-in-Publication data is on file with the
publisher.

Source of Production: Versa Press, East Peoria, Illinois, USA
Date of Production: May 2016
Run Number: 5006620

Printed and bound in the United States of America.
VP 10 9 8 7 6 5 4 3 2 1

To Sabrina Chap, my partner in crime and musicals!

You will always be a FAB chick in my book.

—Sheryl

Team Mickey

Mickey Williams burst into the Fashion Academy of Brooklyn (a.k.a. FAB) with only ten minutes to spare before first period. The school bus had been late this morning, and no matter how hard she willed the traffic to move over the Brooklyn Bridge, it had taken forever. As she dashed to her locker, the halls were buzzing with students who couldn't help but stare at her outfit of the day.

"Ooh-la-la!" JC exclaimed, noting his BFF's Eiffel Tower print T-shirt, cancan-inspired tiered ruffle skirt, and purple studded beret. He could always count on Mickey for an early-morning fashion wake-up call.

"You like?" she asked, giving her ensemble a twirl. She'd paired it with a mismatched pair of combat boots—one purple, one pink. Although she was pressed for time, she was glad she'd run into JC. She had something important to ask him.

"It's certainly very Parisian," JC said. "All you need is a croissant-shaped purse to go with it."

Mickey pulled a gold, rectangular-shaped bag out of her backpack. "Baguette," she said. "I'm one step ahead of you."

"So what's with all the French-ness?" her friend asked.

By now, JC knew that Mickey's personal style was a bit over the top. But it rarely had such a strong theme, much less an international one. Mickey loved to clash her colors and patterns and to stripe her hair with colored chalk to match her ensemble. That had earned her a scholarship to FAB this year—and gotten everyone's attention. And while not everyone embraced her talent for out-of-the-box designs, she and JC had hit it off instantly. He truly appreciated her fierce and fearless fashion attitude.

"Didn't you hear about the International Student Runway?" Mickey replied. Mr. Kaye, her Apparel Arts teacher, had made a really big deal out of it and practically insisted that someone from FAB win—or else. Kaye was never kidding when he issued a command in one of his design classes. He was tough. So tough that rumor had it he used his thumb for a pincushion!

JC raised an eyebrow. "And you wanna win bad. Why?"

Mickey closed her eyes and sighed. "Because the top FAB team gets to go to Paris Fashion

Week and present their designs at the annual FIFI gala. I've always dreamed of going to Paris!"

"FIFI?" JC gasped. "As in the French Institute of the Fashion Industry?"

Mickey nodded. "Amazing, right?"

"Amazing—and near to impossible. Every fashion student in the world is probably competing."

"I know," Mickey said. "Which is why I need your help. I've never been anywhere out of the country, and I don't know anything about Paris— except for what I'm wearing. Oh, and those colorful little sandwich cookies."

"Macarons," JC corrected her. "I've visited Ladurée in France several times."

"You did mention that…several times," Mickey teased. "Something about staying with your cousin Angelique? Eating crepes and shopping on the Champs-Élysées?"

JC nodded. "My cuz moved to France a few years ago. She's very cool—and very fashionable."

Mickey sighed. "Do I have to beg?"

JC's Chihuahua Madonna made a whimpering noise from inside her dog bag.

"Can you top that?" JC snickered.

"JC!"

"Fine. No begging necessary."

"There's just one little thing before you agree," Mickey added.

JC raised his hand to silence her. "Don't tell me. Does it wear a tiara and have a bad attitude?" Of course, he meant FAB's resident Designzilla and queen bee, Jade Lee. If there was a prize to be had, an award to be bestowed, Jade thought she deserved it. Her mother was a hugely popular Hollywood fashion designer, and Jade figured that earned her the right to be a star as well.

Mickey nodded. "Jade is determined to win. She and Jake are partnering up as usual."

Jade's twin brother, Jake, did whatever his sis told him to do—even if it meant trampling his fellow students in the process.

"You think I'm afraid of the tacky twins?" JC

asked. "Pullease. You shouldn't be either. You can't cover up boring with bling. And you... Well, you're one of a kind, Mick."

Mickey blushed. "You really think so? How many times has Jade beaten me on fashion challenges? And how many times has she gotten us in trouble with Mr. Kaye?"

"Too many. Which means she's running out of options. Besides, I bet you were already working up ideas while Jade was out getting her mani and pedi."

"Well, I was thinking of doing a mini collection that draws from the iconic architecture of Paris. The Eiffel Tower, the Arc de Triomphe..."

"Love!" JC cheered. "Tell me more!"

Mickey pulled her sketchbook out of her bag. "It's all pretty rough, but maybe colors that are muted, like grays and blues and black to match the structures. Metallic silver and bronze studding that looks like rivets. And the shape of this skirt—"

She showed him a dramatic A-line gown with a corseted back. "This mimics the lines of the Eiffel Tower."

"Not bad," JC said thoughtfully. "Not bad at all."

"So it's a yes?" Mickey asked.

JC smiled slyly. "Madonna? What do you say to joining Team Mickey?"

Madonna barked happily.

"That's a yes for both for us," JC said. "Paris Fashion Week, here we come."

★ Mr. Kaye's Competition ★

When Mickey got to her Apparel Arts class, Mr. Kaye was already there, snapping his tape measure to get the class's attention.

"Punctuality," he reminded Mickey as she quickly took her seat. "We have a lot to discuss today."

Mickey nodded. "I'm sorry, Mr. Kaye," she said. "JC and I were just so excited talking about the International Student Runway and Paris."

Mr. Kaye gave her outfit the once-over. "So I see. Interesting choices."

Jade's ears suddenly perked up. She was applying lip gloss and quickly tucked her makeup back into her purse. "You and Bowwow Boy are working together? Oh, I'm shaking in my boots!"

Jake peered under the desk. "But you're not wearing boots today," he pointed out. "Those are your platform pumps."

Jade scowled. "Duh, I didn't mean it literally! Clearly I got the brains in this family."

Mickey chuckled. "And I'm sure you and Jake will work *so* well together—since you get along so well."

Mr. Kaye held up a hand to silence them. "You may choose to work in teams, but I warn you that often makes things harder, not easier. And watch the cohesion of your collection: all three looks must embody a French theme, yet each piece must be able to stand on its own."

Gabriel's hand shot up. "Mars and I want to team up," he said. "I'm doing the main outfit, and she's doing all the accessories."

"I have these awesome semiprecious stones that will make the coolest earrings," Mars added. "I'm thinking shoulder dusters! And I'm hammering copper for the stackable bangles."

South sat quietly in her seat, not saying a word.

"South?" Mr. Kaye asked. "Are you working with anyone?"

South shook her head. "My dad made a really difficult decision a few years ago to break up with his hip-hop group and become a solo rap artist. I mean, Diddy and Kanye both advised against it, but he stood his ground."

Mr. Kaye sighed. "And *what* does this have to do with your International Student Runway entry?"

"Nothing. She's just name-dropping," Jade said, stifling a yawn. "Like I care."

"I've decided to go it alone," South replied, shooting Jade a nasty look. "I'm going to be a solo act like my dad."

"That's cool," Gabriel assured her. "I mean, it's easier 'cause there's no one to boss you around."

Mars bristled. "Are you referring to me? Because I am not bossy."

"Really? The outfit needs to be bronze to play up your topaz earrings and bronze bracelets? That's not bossing me around?" Gabriel replied.

"And now you see the challenge of working together as a team," Mr. Kaye said, interrupting them. "When two creative minds get together, there are bound to be fireworks. Expect it. Prepare for it. Deal with it."

He wrote the word MONDAY on the SMART

Board in bold, all-capital, red letters. "That is when your first sketches are due to me."

Jade raised her hand. "That's a week away. Seriously? You want us to come up with a three-piece collection in a week?" She pointed at Jake. "Do you know what I'm dealing with?"

Mr. Kaye brushed her off. "No excuses. Monday, 9:00 a.m. sharp. I can only send one team of students to Paris."

"Or one brilliant student who is going it alone," South pointed out.

"Or one individual student," Mr. Kaye continued. "This competition is *extremely* important. It has to be the best work you have ever done at FAB."

Gabriel scratched his head. "How come? I mean, it's not your fault if FAB doesn't wow those fancy French fashion types."

Mr. Kaye sighed. "I don't want to get into it," he said, waving his hand dismissively. "But I will tell you that you are not the only ones worrying. I also have some stiff competition—at FIFI itself."

Mickey found JC in the cafeteria feeding Madonna scraps of his fish filet under the table.

"That bad, huh?" she asked, taking a sniff of the food on his tray.

"Oh, it's delicious…if you're a dog," he said, groaning. "Next time, remind me to go for the vegetarian plate." Mickey had chosen it: a brightly colored quinoa, cranberry, and squash salad.

"I guess Aunt Olive is rubbing off on me," she said, digging in. Her aunt insisted on a meatless home, and Mickey couldn't argue with her. Not when her aunt had agreed to let her move from Philly and stay with her for the entire school year. Neither Olive nor Mickey's mom were thrilled with the situation, but Mickey knew she had no other choice. If she wanted to be a fashion designer, FAB was the place to be. And if it meant giving up cheeseburgers and chili dogs—not to mention her home and friends back in Philly—then so be it.

Her mind had been made up even before she received the acceptance letter for a full scholarship to FAB. Fashion was her passion and the one thing that made her deliriously happy. From the time she was in kindergarten, she'd always had an eye for style. Her Barbies with their custom Mickey Williams couture looks were proof. But as she got older, she wanted to sew more, be more. As she flipped through the pages of *Vogue* and *Elle*, admiring page after page of exquisite looks, she thought, *My designs will be in here one day.*

And now, she could truly envision herself on that runway during Paris Fashion Week, showing the mini collection she and JC were going to create. She just had to get there.

"So, Mr. Kaye said something really mysterious in class today," Mickey shared with JC.

"And this shocks you? The man is full of surprises. Last week he gave a pop quiz in my History of Zippers class—on Velcro! What does that have to do with zippers?"

"No, this was really weird," Mickey insisted. "Like, personal."

"Well, what did he say?" JC asked.

Mickey tried her best to recall the exact words.

"Something about having stiff competition himself at FIFI."

JC pulled out his laptop and typed in the address for the FIFI website. "Let's see, shall we?" he said, clicking on various tabs. "Whoa, this place looks intense! Check out the course list: The Mechanics of Macramé? The History of Fashion and Civilization?" He scrolled through the photos of the enormous campus until he arrived at the list of faculty.

"Interesting…" he said, reading intently.

"What? What's interesting?" Mickey tried reading over his shoulder.

"They have an Apparel Arts teacher at FIFI too. Monsieur Gaston Roget."

"Ro-jay," Mickey repeated.

"Your French accent…" JC laughed. "We gotta do something about that."

"You think this Mr. Roget is Mr. Kaye's competition?"

JC shrugged. "I think it's a good bet."

Mickey nodded. "Then that's it. We can't lose. We can't let Mr. Kaye down." She pulled out her weekly planner and looked over the dates. "If we work every day after school on the sketches, we should have something to show by next Monday."

"Whoa, every day? You didn't mention that when you recruited me," JC protested. "I have a life, you know."

"Really?" Mickey asked. "What were your plans?"

JC thought hard. "Well, I was going to take Madonna to the groomers tomorrow. And then *Desperately Seeking Susan* is on TV Thursday night…"

Mickey shook her head. "JC, this is much more important. We have to convince Mr. Kaye we're the ones to go to FIFI and present on the international runway."

"And what then?" JC asked. "Have you talked to your mom about this? She wasn't keen on you coming to New York, so what makes you think she'll let you go to Paris?"

Mickey gulped. She really hadn't thought about that. What if her mom freaked out and said no? What if she called Mr. Kaye and told him he had to pick another representative from FAB? It would be mortifying! Mickey quickly pushed the idea out of her head. "We'll cross that bridge when we come to it," she assured JC. "Let's just win first."

"I'm down for it," JC said. "I'm just saying this could open up a whole other can of worms."

Madonna yapped under the table.

"See, Madonna agrees with me," JC said.

"I think Madonna's still hungry and the can of worms sounded good," Mickey teased him.

"Tastier than the lunch here, for sure," JC tossed back.

Mickey picked up her bag and deposited her quinoa bowl on JC's tray. "Better eat up. You'll need your energy. We're starting work on our designs right after school."

Dueling Designers

Mickey dumped a mountain of fabric on Aunt Olive's kitchen table and stood back to admire it.

"What is all this?" JC asked, confused.

"Inspiration," Mickey replied. "Don't you love all these grays and charcoals and… Ooh! This black velvet I got at the flea market last weekend! It's an old coat with some rips, but we can cut it up and repurpose it into something amazing."

JC tapped a finger to the tip of his nose. "Nope. Not feelin' it. Looks like a big, hot mess to me."

"JC!" Mickey wailed. "Could you at least try to use your imagination?" She held up a sheer scrap of gray chiffon. "Doesn't this remind you of Paris at night?"

JC pushed the pile of scraps aside and took out his laptop. "Mick, if you want to be inspired by Paris, then you need to see it." He passed her the computer and clicked on a folder. A slideshow of photos appeared.

"Voilà!" JC said. "Paris by day, Paris by night!"

Mickey looked closely at the screen. "Paris by JC! These are your vacation photos!"

"Oh, here I am with Madonna standing under the Arc de Triomphe," he said, remembering. "And here I am with Madonna at the Louvre Museum."

"No offense to you or your dog, but this is not doing anything to get my creativity flowing," Mickey insisted.

JC slammed his laptop shut. "Fine. You need to embrace the French culture. This instant."

"Here? In New York City?" Mickey asked. "How am I supposed to do that? Order in french fries?"

JC pulled her toward the door. "First stop, the Met Museum to see the works of some of the great French impressionist painters. Then we'll grab some escargot at my mom's favorite little French bistro."

"Wait!" Mickey protested. "Isn't that snails? You want me to eat snails?"

"I want you to understand what the French joie de vivre is all about," JC insisted. "It will really help inspire your designs. Can't you see a hat shaped like a snail shell?"

"But I thought I'd make a dress that drapes like the Eiffel Tower," Mickey said. She was disappointed that JC was already trying to change her design ideas, just like the time he tried to change her into "Kenzie Wills," a faux Finnish fashion socialite. It hadn't worked. In fact, it had only made Jade hate her more.

"You can do whatever your heart desires," JC assured her. "But you asked me to help you create something authentically French. You can't do that unless you do your homework."

He pulled a small green box out of his bag and opened it. Inside were the prettiest pink and purple macarons Mickey had ever seen.

"Have one," he said, waving them under her nose.

"They smell like…like…flowers."

"Roses to be exact. And the purple one is violet."

"The French eat flowers?" Mickey asked, taking

31

a nibble. The cookie was light and sweet with just a hint of rose flavor. She gobbled the rest in one bite.

"The French are about the senses: sights, smells, tastes, textures," JC rattled off.

"Uh-huh," Mickey said with her mouth full. She had helped herself to seconds and thirds. "This is really good."

He opened the door. "Are you coming?" he asked. "I know an amazing little French chocolate shop that gives out free samples."

Mickey grabbed her denim jacket. "Lead the way!"

Once they had eaten several chocolate truffles and stopped to wash them down with a bottle of bubbly French spring water, JC led Mickey to the steps of the Met Museum. The museum was a block long, perched on the edge of Central Park and filled with every kind of art imaginable. As Mickey bounded up the steps and entered the main hall, she had no idea where to go or start. Entire wings were dedicated to different artists, periods, and techniques.

"Ooh, can we start in the Egyptian wing?" she asked, tugging on JC's sleeve.

"Another day," JC said. "We're headed to the French impressionists." He pulled Mickey along after him. "I've been coming here since I was a little kid—so I know where everything is."

Mickey nodded. That was good because she could barely figure out the map the lady at the information booth had handed her.

"I have my favorite paintings," he continued, "but I don't want to influence you. You pick your own." He led her to a section labeled "Art and Modernism."

Mickey wandered around the galleries, trying to absorb it all. There were so many artists' works to take in: Renoir, Manet, Monet, Cézanne, Degas. A plaque on the wall explained that in 1874, a group of artists called the Anonymous Society of Painters, Sculptors, and Printmakers organized an exhibition that launched the entire impressionist movement.

"So they kind of all marched to their own drummer?" Mickey asked, taking it all in. "Cool!" The plaque also pointed out that impressionist paintings were considered shocking and radical to eyes accustomed to more sober colors.

"I bet I would have gotten along great with these guys," she added.

"I love this one—for obvious reasons," JC said, pointing to a Renoir of a young woman dressed in pale blue with a tiny, white dog at her feet. "Now that's a perfectly painted pup."

But something else caught Mickey's eye across the room—something magical.

"What in the world?" she asked, getting closer to a painting of groups of people in a park. When she was almost nose to nose with the painting, all the images of the people, the trees, and the grass became millions of tiny, different-colored dots.

"How do they do that?" Mickey wondered out loud.

A man with a blue beret, a pointy gray beard, and a black eye patch overheard and answered her. "It's a technique called pointillism," he said. "Seurat was the master, no?"

"No… I mean yes!" Mickey said. She noticed that the man had a slight French accent. "I love all the colors and how they blend so seamlessly together into a bigger picture."

"You have a good eye for art," the man said. "I do too. You see?" He pointed to his one good eye and laughed. Then he noticed her outfit. Beneath her jacket, she was still wearing her cancan skirt and mismatched boots. "And for fashion as well?"

"I try." Mickey blushed. "Are you an artist?"

"A teacher." He extended his hand to shake. "I'm Tony."

"I'm Mickey." She motioned toward JC who was still admiring the Cézanne. "My friend brought me here to learn about French art."

"Well," Tony continued. "Your friend is very wise. This is one of the greatest collections of French impressionism in the world."

JC came back to stand beside Mickey and glared at Tony. "And you are?"

"This is JC," Mickey said, introducing her friend. "And this is Tony. He knows so much about pointing-ism."

"Pointillism." Tony chuckled. "The painting technique Seurat uses."

"Yeah, well, good for him." JC sniffed. He

took Mickey by the arm and pulled her toward the gallery exit.

When they were outside on the steps to the museum, Mickey finally had time to catch her breath. "Really, JC? That was so rude!"

"Rude? You promised your aunt Olive you wouldn't talk to strangers. I turn my back for five seconds, and I find you having a whole conversation with Bluebeard the pirate!"

Mickey chuckled. "You are so overly dramatic," she said, patting him on the shoulder. "He was just some nice gentleman who liked French art."

"He looked suspicious to me," JC said. "Like an international art thief. Or a spy!"

"He said he was a teacher. And he did teach me about pointillism. Now I have a great idea for my sketches."

JC smiled. "Why am I not surprised?"

Designs à Deux

When Mickey got to class Monday morning, she couldn't wait to show Mr. Kaye what she and JC had worked on over the weekend. She had so many sketches that her binder was bursting with them.

"Settle down, settle down," Mr. Kaye said as he entered the studio. "I have a splitting headache."

"Uh-oh," Gabriel whispered to her. "This isn't going to be pretty. He's in a bad *m-o-o-d*."

"I can spell," Mr. Kaye said. "And I have extremely sharp hearing."

Mickey gulped. Maybe this wasn't the best time to show him all of her ideas. But it was too late not to.

"Mickey, you're up first. What do you have to present to the class?"

Jade stifled a yawn. "Can we make it quick? The *real* designers here are waiting to show their work."

Mickey stood up and pulled her favorite sketch out of her binder. "This is inspired by a painting called *A Sunday Afternoon on the Island of Le Grande Jatte*. Sunday is my favorite day of the week because Aunt Olive and I go bird-watching in the park. So you can see the feathers on the shoulders and the green dotted fabric…"

Jade wrinkled her nose. "What's with all the polka dots? It looks like your dress has a rash! Poison ivy from the park, maybe?" She elbowed Jake to laugh at her joke.

"Good one, sis!" he chimed in.

"It's a painting technique based on the one used by the French artist Georges Seurat. I'm going to use fabric paints to create a custom textile."

Mr. Kaye nodded. "Interesting concept. And I'm glad you mentioned textiles. Tomorrow, I'm taking you all on a field trip to Plush Fabric in the Fashion District."

"Ooh," Mars said. "Plush is *the* fabric store."

"It is," Mr. Kaye replied. "There are thousands upon thousands of textiles to choose from."

Mickey's hand shot up. "But I kinda wanted to make my own fabric. Would that be okay?"

Jade snickered. "Of course you do. You probably want to use some old sheets you found in the scrap bin—or the garbage. Good luck with that. I'll be buying silk and cashmere."

"You'll be buying or using whatever you want—as long as it doesn't total more than fifty dollars," Mr. Kaye insisted. "Those are the rules of the International Student Runway competition."

"Fifty?" Jade gasped. "That won't even cover my zippers and thread!"

Mr. Kaye rubbed his temples. "Then I suggest you get creative. What are you thinking for your design?"

Jade held up her sketch, and Mickey's mouth dropped. "It's inspired by the architecture of Paris," Jade explained. "The A-line skirt represents the shape of the Eiffel Tower. And the corset back is inspired by the steel crossbeams."

"What? That's what I was doing!" Mickey

protested. She pulled out several other sketches from her binder.

"Well, I thought of it first," Jade insisted.

"You did not!" Mickey fired back. "You must have seen my sketches or heard me talking to JC and copied."

Jade laughed. "Me? Copy? As if! I've been to Paris dozens of times, and I know the architecture inside and out."

Mr. Kaye held up his hand. "Ladies, ladies! Enough bickering. Brilliant minds sometimes think alike. One of you will simply have to rethink your collection, or you'll both be out of the running."

Mickey texted JC to meet her after Apparel Arts. She could barely contain her anger.

"It's so unfair!" she shouted the minute she spotted him making his way toward her locker. "Jade stole my whole Paris architecture idea."

"Do you want my opinion?" JC asked.

Mickey rolled her eyes. "Am I gonna like it?"

"Your idea was, well, not all that original, Mick. I mean, everyone will probably design collections based on the Eiffel Tower. It's almost a cliché."

Mickey paused to consider. "Ya think?"

"I think we can do better. What about that sketch you love? The green dots?"

"I know, I do love the pointillism dress," she said. "But Jade said it looked like a rash. I can't do a whole collection covered in dots."

"And since when do we care what other people think?" JC reminded her.

"I know, but it is a bit much—even for me," Mickey said. "And it would take forever to paint enough fabric for three looks. We only have a week."

"Okay," JC said, taking his sketchbook out of his bag. "So maybe you do one dress inspired by Seurat and one jacket inspired by Renoir." He showed her a drawing he'd made in the museum of a coat covered in broad, loose brushstrokes. On the back was an image of the white dog from the painting. "I can draw dogs in my sleep."

"Stunning!" Mickey said, grabbing the sketch out of his hands. "And brilliant."

JC blushed. "Why, yes, I am." A yap came from inside his bag. "And Madonna seconds that."

Mickey giggled. "I meant the design. So we just need a third look inspired by a French artist, and we're good to go."

"You should thank Jade," JC added. "She just pushed you to come up with an even better idea."

Mickey crossed her fingers. "Let's hope it's good enough to beat Team Jade."

5

Frenemies

Mickey had never been to Plush Fabric. So when Mr. Kaye ushered them through the doors, her jaw dropped. She felt like she was in Disney World! She had never seen so many bolts of beautiful material and could barely contain her excitement.

"You'll find it's organized by section," Mr. Kaye explained. "Cottons and silks downstairs; wools and jersey upstairs."

"Velvet?" South asked. "Where do I find velvet?" A polite saleswoman wearing a pair of scissors on a string around her neck directed South to the back of the first floor.

"We need some vegan leather," Mars reminded Gabriel. "Chocolate brown." A salesman showed them the section upstairs.

Mickey wandered up and down the aisles, snipping off swatches of assorted colors so she could compare them. Jade snuck up behind her. In fact, she'd been following Mickey around the entire time, just waiting to pounce.

"Are we making a patchwork quilt?" Jade asked, snatching a square of blue cotton out of

Mickey's basket. "What's with all this mess? And ick! Is this polyester?"

Before Mickey could respond, Jake jumped between her and Jade. "You have to see this silver metallic taffeta I found," he told his sister. "It's perfect!"

Jade's eyes narrowed. She was having fun taunting Mickey—and Jake had ruined it. "Really? Haven't I told you *never* to interrupt me when I'm in the middle of something?"

"But it's gorgeous—and really expensive!" Jake replied. He'd said the magic word.

"Expensive? How expensive?" Jade asked excitedly. "I love expensive!" She forgot all about Mickey and wandered off with her brother.

Mickey looked down at her basket, filled with multicolored scraps. She had no idea what to do for her third look—a romper? A pantsuit? A moto jacket? And what color should she choose? Maybe Jade was right. It did look like a big mess.

"You look perplexed," said a voice behind her.

Mickey expected to see a salesman—but it was Tony from the museum!

"Hey!" she said, smiling.

"We meet again," he replied, bowing ever so slightly. "May I offer some assistance?"

"Actually, you could," Mickey said. "I'm

designing a mini collection based on three French painters: Seurat, Renoir, and I have no idea."

"Never heard of Monsieur 'I have no idea,'" Tony teased.

"I need a third one," Mickey clarified. "But I don't know enough about French art to be inspired."

"I see," Tony said. "Tell me about yourself—as a fashion designer."

Mickey wrinkled her nose and thought hard. "Well, I don't try to design like anyone else," she said. "I guess you would say my looks are a little out of the box?"

Tony took his phone out of his pocket and pulled up a photo of a boldly painted still life.

The blue teapot and yellow and orange fruit practically jumped out of their canvas. "Like this, perhaps?"

Mickey studied the painting. "The colors are so bright and powerful," she said.

"*Oui*. Gauguin was thought to be very avant-garde in his time."

Mickey nodded. "So people didn't get him?"

"Get him?" Tony looked confused. "Ah, *oui*! They didn't understand or appreciate his art—not for quite some time. While everyone was doing soft, muted colors, he chose to paint in brights. His paintings had great symbolism and inspired many painters who followed."

Mickey studied the painting. "I like him. He's inspiring me." She waved at Mr. Kaye who was across the floor. "Where are the fluorescent fabrics?"

Mr. Kaye's eyes grew wide. She wasn't sure what she had said to upset him, but he came charging toward her with steam coming out of his ears. Then she realized he wasn't heading for her at all. He was about to grab Tony!

"Gaston Roget!" he shouted.

"Chester Kaye," Tony replied.

Mickey stared. What was he talking about? Tony had been so nice—and helpful! Then she remembered the name JC had found on the FIFI website—the name of the Apparel Arts teacher and Mr. Kaye's big competitor. She looked at Tony and realized that without the eye patch, beard, and graying hair, her museum buddy did look slightly familiar.

"Why are you bothering one of my students?" Mr. Kaye continued yelling at him.

"I was merely helping," Tony replied.

"Helping? Helping her to lose the International Student Runway competition is more likely," Mr. Kaye fired back.

He turned to Mickey. "Mackenzie. Leave us— at once!"

Mickey gulped. She had never seen Mr. Kaye

this angry. She backed off and ducked behind a few bolts of fabric where she could hear everything and see the two of them face each other, nose to nose.

"Such a lovely treat seeing you again, *mon ami*!" Tony smiled slyly.

"Don't you '*mon ami*' me," Mr. Kaye replied. "You're no friend."

"Ah, but you forget. We were the best of friends once. A long, long time ago."

"Ancient history!" Mr. Kaye snapped. "You are nothing but a slimy, underhanded, conniving…"

"Tsk-tsk." Tony waved his pointer finger in Mr. Kaye's face. "It's not polite to call people names."

"And it's not polite to steal people's jobs," Mr. Kaye said. "You knew I wanted the position at FIFI."

"And you found yourself a job here instead—in Brooklyn."

Mr. Kaye's face was now bright red. "Because you stole my job."

"Stole? That is a very harsh word. I would say I just pointed out to the administration that I was the better candidate."

"Better? You will never be a better teacher than me!" Mr. Kaye insisted.

Mickey didn't know what to do or say—but she had to defend Mr. Kaye somehow.

"He is!" she said, jumping out of her hiding spot. "He's the best teacher. He knows everything about fashion design, and he's helped me find my voice as a designer."

Tony smiled. "Good for you. You see, Chester, you are just where you should be. Who needs Paris?"

Mr. Kaye gritted his teeth. "My students will win the runway competition this year, and you will eat your words," he vowed.

Tony smiled. "Then I wish you well. May the best teacher win." With that, he turned and left Plush.

"Mr. Kaye…are you okay?" Mickey asked gently.

"Why were you fraternizing with the enemy?" he bellowed.

"The enemy? Tony didn't seem like the enemy. He seemed like a nice guy."

"He's a liar and a thief," Mr. Kaye answered. "A wolf in sheep's clothing!"

Once again, she had no idea what her teacher was going on and on about—so she just nodded her head in agreement. "I can see you don't like each other very much."

Mr. Kaye took a deep breath. "He is not to be trusted. I don't know why he's here in New York, but it's no doubt to sabotage me."

Mickey actually liked Tony's idea about

Gauguin's bold colors, but she could never tell Mr. Kaye where it had come from. "I'm just going to find some fluorescent-pink and green silks," she said. Mr. Kaye didn't even hear her. He was still mumbling to himself—something about "a barracuda with no taste or style."

Mickey noticed Jade pushing Jake toward a display of buttons and trims. "Not *those* buttons. Honestly, do you have *any* taste that's not in your mouth?" Jade asked her brother.

Jade realized then that Mickey was watching her. "Yoo-hoo, Mickey! The burlap is in the basement," Jade called to her. "And the bargain bin: twenty-five cents a yard!"

Mickey realized she knew exactly how Mr. Kaye felt. Tony was his Jade Lee! As much as Mickey tried to ignore them, the snarky remarks and mean jabs hurt—and they chipped away at her confidence.

She looked back at Mr. Kaye and knew she had only one option: to win for both of them.

6

If at First You Don't Succeed...

Mickey had spent nearly all weekend staring at her dress form, Edith. She'd named her after the famous Hollywood designer, Edith Head. But now neither she—nor Edith—looked particularly happy with the result of her design. It was a simple halter-top jumpsuit, covered in assorted neon fabric squares, arranged in a woven, checkered pattern. All she could think about was what Jade had said—"Are you making a patchwork quilt?"—because that's what her design looked like.

Aunt Olive came in Mickey's bedroom and rested a plate of kale cookies and a cup of chamomile tea on her nightstand.

"Tough assignment?" she asked. "You've been at it all day."

Mickey sighed. "Impossible. I just can't see it."

Olive looked at Edith. "I think it's too tidy." Coming from her aunt—a legal secretary and neat freak who believed in moderation, precision, and exacting detail—that sounded strange.

"Too tidy?" Mickey asked.

Olive chose her words carefully. "I think it feels like you're trying too hard."

Mickey rested her head on her desk. She knew Olive was right. She *was* trying too hard. The design wasn't flowing like it usually did. She was thinking too much about what people would say when they saw it—and not about what she wanted to say as a designer.

"I'm calling JC," Mickey finally said. "He's my partner on this project, and I need his advice."

She used FaceTime on her phone so her friend could get a look at what she'd created.

"A little more to the right…no the left," JC said as she held up her phone to Edith's outfit.

"Now back up," JC added. "Way, way up. Can you leave the room?"

"Leave the room?" Mickey asked. "Why?"

"It's just… Well, it's not working. It looks like something I finger-painted in kindergarten! Wait…are those bell-bottoms? Eek! It keeps getting worse!"

"JC!" Mickey moaned. "You're making *me* feel worse!"

"I'm sorry. I'm just being honest," he replied. "You called me for my opinion."

Mickey nodded. "I did. So what do you think?"

"I think you should shred that outfit and start all over," JC suggested. "Doesn't your aunt have one of those document shredders for work?"

Mickey gritted her teeth. "Not helping." Then an idea came to her. "Wait! That's it."

"What's *it*?" JC asked.

"Shred it! I should shred it!"

"Uh, yeah. Back to the ol' drawing board."

"No, I mean literally!"

JC looked confused. "When you get that crazy look in your eye, I should just get out of your way and let you get down to designing."

Mickey wasn't even listening; she had already started taking a scissor to the pant legs of Edith's outfit.

"Okay, Mick. *Bon chance!* That's French for good luck!" He clicked off his phone.

Mickey took a step back to admire her new idea. "Edith, we have a winner!" she said excitedly. "I can't wait to show Mr. Kaye tomorrow."

7

Show-and-Tell

When the first-period bell rang, Mickey dashed into Advanced Apparel Arts, dragging a huge garment bag over her shoulder. JC trailed behind her, rolling in Edith who was covered in a drape cloth.

"Whoa," South said as Mickey took the seat next to her. "Whatcha got in the bag?"

"Something I'm really proud of," Mickey answered. "It took me a long time, but I think it's one of my best designs."

Jade shot her a look from across the studio. "That isn't saying much," she commented before taking out a compact to powder her nose. "Your best is at best...mediocre."

JC sprang to her defense. "Why don't you wait and see before you make your nasty little comments," he said. "You might be eating those words."

Jade didn't bother looking away from her own reflection. "Whatevs."

"They don't stand a chance. Right, Jade?" Jake asked, looking for reassurance. "I mean, our design is *sick*."

"Sick? Who's sick?" Mr. Kaye asked. It wasn't

like him to be a minute late, but today he seemed to be dragging. "Silence!" he bellowed at the class. Then he sneezed and coughed and dabbed his bright-red nose with a hankie. "I'm sick as a dog—and do I have one of you to blame for it?"

The students all shook their heads no. There wasn't a single sniffle—besides his—in the studio.

"My head is pounding. My throat is raw," he said. "I'm sure it's the flu—or the plague. You!" he snapped at Gabriel. "Present!"

Gabriel and Mars quickly rolled their dress form to the front of the room. "Our collection is inspired by Paris's underground sewers," Gabriel began.

"Ew!" Jade cried. "That's disgusting!"

"Gross!" Jake chimed in. "Isn't that place filled with whatever you flush?"

Mr. Kaye tried to silence the class but launched into a coughing fit instead.

Mars spoke for him. "Would you please keep your comments to yourselves till after the presentation?" she told Jake and Jade. "Zip it!"

Gabriel thought she was talking to him and quickly zipped the black velvet hoodie they'd designed. "See? The shape of the hood mimics the shape of the sewer tunnels," he said.

"And we've accessorized it with a chain-link skirt that I welded," Mars said.

"Very—*achoo!*—innovative," Mr. Kaye said. "And what does the rest of your collection look like?"

Gabriel pulled out a motorcycle jacket constructed from gray flannel with silver studs and a brown satin trench coat that Mars had embellished with a huge, gold skull-shaped brooch.

"It's a bit dark," Mr. Kaye said, squinting to get a better look at the pieces. "Then again, my vision is somewhat hazy today…"

Jade's hand shot up. "Can I show mine now? It'll make you feel better."

Mr. Kaye sneezed. "Fine. You're next."

Jade and Jake wheeled the dress figure to

the front of the room. It was draped in a red velvet cloth. "Be prepared for brilliance," Jade said, as she triumphantly yanked the cloth away. "Ta-da!"

Mr. Kaye didn't look very wowed—in fact, he looked half asleep! But Mickey's heart sank. As much as she hated to admit it, Jade's design was pretty amazing.

"I used black leather strips to create the image of the Eiffel Tower," she said, rolling the silver, silk column gown close to Mr. Kaye so he could get a better look. "The crisscross lattice pattern you see? All hand-stitched."

"Not by *her* hand," JC muttered under his

breath. "Her mommy's seamstresses probably did it for her."

"And this," Jake said, "is my tuxedo jacket inspired by the architectural plans for the tower. The fabric is actually printed with a copy of the real blueprints."

Mickey was utterly speechless. Why hadn't she thought of that?

Jade snapped her fingers at Mr. Kaye to make sure he was still awake. He jumped to attention and scowled.

"Just one more thing," she said. "My Arc de Triomphe trousers!" She pulled out a pair of pants from her garment bag. Each leg was embroidered to look like one of the arch's neo-classical columns.

Mr. Kaye raised an eyebrow. "Your collection is well executed and well thought-out," he said hoarsely. "But I fear it's a bit literal."

Jade's face flushed. "Literal? I *literally* created a masterpiece. Three of them, to be exact!"

Mr. Kaye continued. "I think you could have pushed the envelope more," he said dismissively. "I'm not sure I see much of you in this collection. I see Paris, but where is Jade?"

Jake elbowed his sister. "See! I told you the blueprint idea was too much. But do you ever listen to me? Nooooo!"

Jade stomped back to her seat, furious.

"South, you went solo. Let's see what you came up with," Mr. Kaye said, popping a cough drop in his mouth.

"I was inspired by French history," South said. "In particular, Queen Marie Antoinette."

Her first look was a modern take on a ruffled royal ball gown—but the skirt was short in the front and long in the back, and pearls were draped dramatically off each cap-sleeved shoulder. Her second design was a gold brocade jean jacket. Instead of studs, big faux diamonds fastened the pockets.

"And last but not least," South said, "I call this

look, 'Let them eat cake!'" She presented a white velvet cape "iced" with pink rickrack trim.

Mr. Kaye cleared his throat. "Nice choice of materials and whimsical designs," he said. "But the execution is a bit sloppy." He pointed to a section of the cape where the trim was hanging loose.

South looked disappointed when she sat back down. "I really thought he was going to love it," she said to Mickey.

"And last but not least, Mickey and company," Mr. Kaye said, punctuating his sentence with a loud *achoo*!

JC ducked for cover. "Hey!" he said, checking his jacket sleeve for any smudges. "This thing took me hours!" He carefully modeled his impressionist-inspired jacket while fiercely protecting it. When Gabriel reached out to feel the fabric, JC yanked the jacket away. "Uh, uh, uh," he warned. "The art is for looking, not touching!"

He then spun around so Mr. Kaye could see the portrait he'd recreated on the back.

"Renoir?" Mr. Kaye asked. "I don't recall the dog in that painting being so pasty white."

JC went back to his seat, returned the jacket to its bag, and bit his tongue. "He's just grumpy because he thinks Monsieur Roget gave you some pointers," he whispered to Mickey. "Don't let him scare you. He's all bark, no bite."

Mickey was up next. She walked to the front of the room, unzipped the garment bag, and pulled out her Seurat wrap dress. "From a distance, we see a lovely park scene of trees and grass," she said. "But up close, it's actually several different shades of green fabric paint applied with a teeny, tiny brush."

Mr. Kaye sniffed. "Yes, yes, go on."

She lifted her third design carefully out of the bag, and Mr. Kaye's face lit up.

"Good heavens!" he said. "What is that?"

"A Gauguin still-life evening gown," Mickey explained. "I mimicked his long, bold brush-strokes by creating floor-length shreds of bright blue, yellow, orange, and green silk. The orange beading around the high neckline is a nod to his painted fruit."

Mr. Kaye dabbed his eyes. Mickey couldn't tell if the cold was making them water or if he was actually moved by what she'd created.

"Creative, innovative, groundbreaking," Mr. Kaye said.

JC elbowed her. "He means you."

"I'll need some time to look at all the work closely and make up my mind, but I do think the winner is fairly evident from today's presentations." He picked up his box of tissues. "Now if you'll excuse me, I'm going to the school nurse."

Mickey couldn't stop smiling. Mr. Kaye had actually loved her designs. All her hard work had paid off. All she had to do was wait for Mr. Kaye to make the big announcement, and she and JC would be going to Paris!

"Don't count your chickens till they've hatched," Jade warned, pushing past her. "This isn't over yet."

8

★ And the Winner Is... ★

Mr. Kaye was absent more than a week with the flu, and Mickey couldn't stand the suspense. When was he going to make the announcement?

"You should put it out of your mind," JC said. "Just forget about it."

"Are you kidding me? It's all I can think about!" Mickey said. "I've always dreamed of going to Paris."

"It's just another big city," JC said, trying to

assure her. "With really chic people, amazing food, breathtaking sights…"

"Ugh!" Mickey sighed. "I wish he'd just get better and get back here!"

Her wish was granted Tuesday morning when she saw Mr. Kaye coming up the steps to the sixth floor. He still looked pale, but at least he wasn't coughing and sneezing his head off!

"Mr. Kaye!" she said, pushing JC out of the way. "You're here! Does that mean…"

Her teacher held up his hand. "I will make the announcement over the loudspeaker before day's end," he told her. "Patience, Mickey, patience."

Patience was not one of Mickey's talents. She

stared at the clock in every class, counting down the hours until the end of the day. When it was last period, she'd almost given up. Then the loudspeaker crackled and came to life.

"Good afternoon, FAB students," Mr. Kaye's voice boomed over it. "I know you've all been waiting for my decision: who will be joining me at the International Student Runway competition in Paris over spring break. After much careful contemplation while I was home in my sickbed, I've decided to award this very special honor to two students who showed creativity, flawless workmanship, and above all the essence of what is FAB…"

Mickey held her breath and crossed her fingers and toes.

"Without further ado, congratulations, Mickey Williams and JC Cumberland!"

Mickey jumped out of her seat and screamed. "Oh my gosh! Oh my gosh! Oh my gosh!" She danced around Mr. Evans's Embellishments class, tossing trim and fabric in the air, completely forgetting she was in the middle of a skills studio lab.

JC raced into the room. "Did you hear him? Did you hear what he said?"

Mr. Evans smiled and gave them both a high five. "Congrats, you two. I'm sure it was well deserved."

When she left school that afternoon, Mickey felt like she was walking on air. It was too good to be true! Then her phone buzzed in her pocket.

"Mickey Mouse!" her mom said when she answered. "How's my girl?"

"Fine, fine," Mickey said. She wanted to blurt out her good news, but thought it would be better to ease into it. If there was one thing her mom hated, it was surprises. She had been furious when Mickey applied to FAB without telling her. And now, this…

"So, Mom," she began. "Are you sitting down?" She could picture her mom standing behind the makeup counter at Wanamaker's department store in Philly, dressed in her black smock and sensible shoes.

"Let me pull up a stool… Why?"

"It's good news. Great news!" Mickey explained. "The greatest news of my whole life!"

"Mickey…" her mom said, already suspicious. "What did you do?"

"I won a design competition at school! I get to go to Paris!"

Mickey waited for her mother to say something, anything.

"Hello? Mom? Did you hear me?" she asked meekly.

"I did."

Mickey feared there was a lecture coming—or worse, a stern "You're grounded, and you're not going anywhere" speech.

"Mom, why aren't you yelling?" Mickey asked.

"Because I'm so thrilled for you!" her mother finally replied. "It was always my dream to go to Paris, and I never quite made it because life got in the way. Oh, Mickey, this is wonderful."

Mickey stared at the screen on her phone. Had she heard right? Was her mom actually happy for her and giving her the okay?

"Sooo, I can go…with JC and Mr. Kaye?"

"I'll have to get all the details, but yes, you can go. How could you *not* go to Paris?"

Mickey hung up and headed for the corner to wait with the other students for the bus back over the Brooklyn Bridge to Manhattan. A white limousine pulled up right in front of her, and someone rolled down the window.

"Bonjour!" Jade said.

Mickey looked around. Was Jade speaking to her?

"I heard that you and Bowwow Boy are going to Paris. Oh, goody."

Mickey was confused. Was Jade congratulating her?

"Um, yeah. Thanks?"

Jade smiled slyly. "It'll be even more fun to beat you there than here."

"Beat me? What do you mean? You're not going to the International Student Runway competition, Jade."

"Oh, aren't I?" she replied. "My mom made some calls to her dear friend, the headmaster of FIFI, and Jake and I will be allowed to compete as an independent team."

Mickey felt her cheeks burn. "Wait a sec—let me get this straight. Your mom bribed FIFI to let you into the competition? When Mr. Kaye didn't pick you?"

"I wouldn't call it a bribe—more like a little favor. Since Mommy just paid for the new Lee Library at FIFI and all."

"Unbelievable!" Mickey shouted at her. "You don't give up, do you?"

Jade's face turned dead serious. "And I won't. Not until you learn there's room for only one design diva at FAB—and it's not you."

9

Plan of Attack

Mr. Kaye met with Mickey and JC the next day after school to outline their game plan for the competition.

"It's not as simple as you might think," their teacher warned them. "Everyone competing is the top of their class. The designs will be impeccable. And you have to create an additional look right there at the runway."

"What? Another look?" Mickey asked. "I thought we just had to do our three."

"We won't find out what it is till we get to Paris," Mr. Kaye explained. "Each team will be given an envelope containing their theme—and you'll have just a few short days to execute it."

Mickey shook her head. "What if the theme is awful? Or we can't find the right fabric for it. What if it's a design disaster?"

"They prefer to call it '*l'ultime défi*' or 'the ultimate challenge,'" Mr. Kaye replied.

"It's the ultimate headache," JC grumped. "Sure we can't get a little hint ahead of time?"

"Absolutely not!" Mr. Kaye said with a huff. "You will find out when we get there, and you will make the most of it. In the meantime…" He handed Mickey and JC a sheet of numbers and a stack of photos. "Here are your models and their specific measurements."

"Wait! What if our designs don't fit them?" Mickey gasped.

"They may not. You'll need to alter them so they do. Welcome to the real world of the runway. You'll have just one day to fit them there."

JC looked the measurements over. "Are you kidding me? All these model have shoulders like linebackers! There's no way my jacket will fit. And—OMG!—the shortest one is almost six feet tall. Mickey's gown will be way too short."

"I'm not too sure how the green dress will work

on this model's skin tone," Mickey questioned. "Maybe she needs some blue or even yellow in it? I thought I was done painting."

"You are far from done." Mr. Kaye said, addressing both of them. "We leave in four weeks, and you'll be working night and day and every Tuesday and Wednesday after school with me, refining your designs till I say they're ready. Impressing me was just the first step. Impressing the French judges...that's something entirely different."

Mickey's mom called that night to check up on her. "How is my designing daughter doing?" she teased.

"Okay, I guess," Mickey replied. "I have so much work to do."

"Just think," her mom reminded her. "In a few weeks you'll be in Paris, strolling the Champs-Élysées, touring le Tour Eiffel…"

Mickey remembered how her mom had said she always wanted to go to Paris, but "life got in the way."

"I wish you could go," she said softly.

"Me too," her mom replied. "Wouldn't that be something?"

Mickey thought her mother sounded a little sad.

"But, hey"—her mom tried to brighten the mood—"you'll take tons of pictures, and it'll be like I was there all along."

"You bet," Mickey promised. But she couldn't help feeling bad. Her mom had always made so many sacrifices for her. She rarely ever took a day off for herself, much less a vacation to Europe.

"Don't you worry about me," her mom insisted. "You just go to Paris and you wow them. And have a few pastries for me while you're at it."

The next day, when Mickey met with Mr. Kaye to go over her revisions, it was obvious to her teacher that she had been distracted.

"This measurement is off," he scolded her. "It's an inch too long for the model's inseam. Do you know how that will look on the runway? *Que'lle horreur!*"

Mickey sighed. "I'm sorry! I thought I double-checked it. I guess my mind wasn't on it last night."

"And where was your mind?" Mr. Kaye fumed. "It should only be on your work."

"I talked to my mom, and she sounded so sad. She's always wanted to go to Paris, and she couldn't because she had to take care of me."

"It sounds like a noble choice," Mr. Kaye replied.

"Well, yes. But it isn't fair to her," Mickey said. "She does everything for me. She always puts me first."

Mr. Kaye nodded. "That is what parents do." He pointed to the dropped stitch on her dress hem. "But that's no excuse for sloppy sewing. Fix it."

Mickey nodded and made herself yet another promise: One day she would take her mom to Paris. One day she'd make her proud.

Up in the Air

The flight left for Paris's Charles de Gaulle Airport at night, and the entire trip, Mr. Kaye snored while JC watched Madonna videos on his iPad. His own Madonna sat in her dog bag, tucked under his feet, snoring as well. Mickey, however, couldn't do anything but look out the window and check her watch.

"You know we won't get there any faster if you stare at the second hand, right?" JC teased.

"Seriously, Mick. Take a snooze. I always get in at least a few hours. When you wake up, we'll be there."

"Nuh-uh," Mickey said. "I'm not missing a second of this trip. I've never flown this far before. The only place my mom and I ever went on a plane was Disney World."

"In my humble opinion, Paris is better than Disney World," JC said. "It's the most magical place on Earth—for a designer, that is."

Mickey leaned back and tried to close her eyes and dream about it—but it was impossible. Instead, she flipped on the overhead light and began reading her *French in Five Minutes a Day* book.

"I figure the flight is about seven hours, so that should get me through almost every chapter," she said, showing JC the cover.

"*Oui!* You'll be fluent by the time we land," he said, chuckling.

Somewhere between studying "*Je m'appelle* Mickey Williams" and the days of the week, she drifted off to the loveliest of dreams. In it, she was strolling along Avenue Montaigne, window-shopping the high-end couture boutiques. She was wearing mirrored Dior So Real sunglasses and a chic YSL leopard-print minidress.

"You!" A voice suddenly shattered the beautiful

image. "You're a fake and a phony, and you don't belong here!"

It was Jade, and she had a group of fancy French girls following at her Louboutin heels. On Jade's command, they all began to point and laugh at Mickey—and chase her down the street.

In the dream, Mickey started running as fast as she could, trying to escape Jade and her evil entourage.

"Go away! Leave me alone!" Mickey shouted at them. "I belong here as much as you do!"

Then she felt a hand reach out and grab her shoulder. "No!" she screamed. "Let me go!"

"Mick, wake up! You're having a nightmare."

JC gave her a gentle nudge. "And from the sounds of it, it's a doozy!"

Mickey opened her eyes and realized she was still on the plane.

"Oh," she said, breathing a sigh of relief. "Sorry. It just felt like it was really happening."

JC nodded. "I once had this dream that Madonna asked me to come onstage and sing with her. My mom said I was singing 'Ray of Light' in my sleep."

The flight attendant checked on their row. "Everything okay here?" she asked. "We'll be landing in about two hours."

Amazingly, even though Mr. Kaye was seated

next to them, he'd managed to sleep through the whole commotion—not to mention dinner, snack, and now breakfast.

"I'm good," Mickey said, getting back to her French book. But she couldn't shake the feeling that Jade Lee was going to be trouble, even three thousand miles from FAB.

Qu'elle Surprise!

When they got to the hotel, Mickey was too exhausted to even unpack.

"Told you to sleep on the plane," JC scolded her. "Now you're going to sleep the day away instead of seeing the sights with me and my cousin Angelique."

"I'll catch up with you later," Mickey said, yawning. "I just need to take a little nap."

Mr. Kaye handed her a room key. "My room

is right next door," he said. "And you are not to leave unescorted by a chaperone. Is that clear?"

Mickey nodded. "I'm not going anywhere. I'm totally lost with all this French. I thought *sortie* was something you do to your laundry— not an exit."

"And I'll be a few block away at my cousin's flat," JC reminded her. "In case you need a translator."

Mickey opened her door and rolled her bag inside.

"Surprise!" her mom shouted, swooping her into a huge bear hug.

"Mom? Am I dreaming? Are you here? *How* are you here?"

"Mr. Kaye arranged everything—my flight, our room, our meals," her mom explained. "I had some vacation time coming at work, so I just took it!"

Mickey gulped. "But, Joanna…" She only called her mom by her first name when she was trying to sound serious and mature. "How can we afford it?"

Her mother smiled. "I'm going to do makeup on the models for the competition next weekend. Mr. Kaye got FIFI to hire me. I'm an official makeup artist for the runway!"

Mickey flopped down on the couch. "He did? That's so awesome," she said, closing her eyes.

"I promise I'll be really excited and remember to thank him when I'm not so tired. Mom, I'm so glad you're here."

Her mom covered Mickey with a blanket and kissed her on the forehead. "Me too. Get some zzz's, Mickey Mouse," she said. "And when you wake up, we're hitting Paris!"

By the time Mickey finally opened her eyes again, it was late afternoon.

"Did I miss it?" she said, yawning.

"Miss what?" her mom asked. She was busy

cleaning her makeup brushes and organizing her eye shadows into palettes.

"I dunno. Paris."

Joanna smiled. "Hardly. Mr. Kaye said we're to meet him in the lobby at four. He's got something up his sleeve, I'm sure."

When they got downstairs, JC was already there with Madonna on a rhinestone-studded leash.

"Bonsoir, sleepyhead," he teased. "The jet lag really got to you, huh?"

"I hate that I slept through half a day," Mickey said. "I didn't want to miss a single moment."

"And you won't," Mr. Kaye said, arriving in

the lobby. "The competition booked us a Paris city tour ending with a bateau on the Seine."

Mickey dug her pocket French dictionary out of her bag. "What's a bateau? And what's a Seine?"

"It's a dinner cruise on the river," JC explained. "I've done one before, and it's great—you can see everything from the water. And they serve crepes for dessert!" Madonna barked her approval.

"Mr. Kaye," Mickey began, "about my mom… I can't thank you enough."

"*De rien*, you're welcome." He waved it off. "It's hard to find a good makeup artist these days." He looked at Mickey's mom and winked.

"Do you think we can climb to the top of the Eiffel Tower?" Joanna asked.

"I believe that is the final stop," Mr. Kaye said, ushering them out the hotel's revolving door. "After you."

The tour bus was packed with fashion students from all over the world and their teachers and chaperones, all chattering in different languages.

"Do you think we stand a chance?" Mickey whispered to JC. "Against all these kids?"

JC scanned the crowd. "*Mais bien sûr!* But of course!" he said. "What do they have that we don't—besides some really crazy foreign accents?"

The rest of the day was filled with seeing the

sights, sampling delicious French pastries, and "*Mais bien sûr!*" a visit to the Eiffel Tower.

Mickey stood next to her mom, looking down on Paris and all its splendor. The city shimmered with a million lights, and the crowds of people below looked like tiny bugs swarming on the street.

"It's so beautiful," her mom said with tears in her eyes. "I never thought I would get to see it."

Mickey squeezed her hand. "When I'm a big-time fashion designer, I'll make sure we go to Paris every year for Fashion Week," she promised. "This is just the beginning, Mom. You'll see."

"I believe you," her mom replied. "And I believe *in* you, Mickey Mouse."

After dinner, Mr. Kaye took JC and Mickey aside for a stern talk. "I know today was a lot of excitement and fun," he said. "But tomorrow it's time to get down to business. We begin at FIFI at 8:00 a.m. sharp, and you'll be receiving the details of *l'ultime défi*."

Mickey gulped. What if she got the hardest challenge? What if she and JC couldn't think of a single look to make? What if they made something that was completely *awful*? Mr. Kaye read her mind: "It will be fine, Mickey. Just focus and have faith in yourself and your abilities. That's what got you here."

Mickey managed a weak smile. There was just so much at stake! Not only her reputation, but Mr. Kaye's and FAB's as well. She tried to remember what her mom always told her: "Winning isn't everything. It's how you play the game." Maybe that worked for elementary school gym class, but this was the big time: Paris! FIFI! The best and brightest fashion schools from around the world!

Her mind was racing that night when she went to bed in the hotel—and not even ordering a cup of warm milk from room service helped. She'd made a promise to her mom and herself that this would not be the last time they came to Paris. But what if it was? What if the students in the competition laughed at her, just like Jade and the French girls in her dream? What if FIFI thought she had no future as a designer? What then?

"Do you remember what I used to do when you were little and couldn't sleep?" her mom asked her.

"Yell, 'Mickey, go to sleep'?" Mickey joked.

"No, I used to sing you a lullaby," her mom replied. "Remember?"

Mickey racked her brain. Then all at once, it came to back to her.

"It was French!" she said. "Something about a boy named Jack?"

Her mom smiled and began to sing softly:

"*Frère Jacques, Frère Jacques. Dormez-vous? Dormez-vous?*"

By the time she reached the part of the song with morning bells ringing "Ding ding dong," Mickey was fast asleep.

12

★ The Ultimate Challenge ★

FIFI was the opposite of FAB. Instead of halls filled with students laughing and chatting and comparing their sketches, it was so quiet you could hear a pin drop. As they tiptoed around, Mickey kept one eye out for Jade. It would be just like her to arrive early and get a jump on the competition.

"They take themselves very seriously here," Mr. Kaye said, holding a finger to his lips. "No

talking above a whisper while class is in session."
He looked around and marveled, "Amazing. It's
exactly the same. Even the *Silence, s'il vous plait*
signs everywhere."

JC rolled his eyes. "You're kidding, right? Who
would want to go to a school like this where you
have to keep quiet all the time?"

"I would. Or did," Mr. Kaye replied. "A
long, long time ago, I attended classes at FIFI,
and it was the only place in the world I wanted
to be."

"So why did you leave?" Mickey asked.

"I didn't have a choice," Mr. Kaye said. He
sounded both angry and sad. "The job I thought

I would have here after college, the job I always wanted, went to someone else."

"You mean Tony the phony?" JC asked him.

"Gaston. Yes. We were once great friends, not unlike the two of you."

"So what happened?" Mickey said. "Did you have a fight?"

"Not a fight, really. He just didn't play fair. He was too afraid I'd overshadow him."

"Sound like any Designzilla we know?" JC elbowed Mickey. "Jade's obviously been taking lessons from the Tony playbook."

"Regardless, I found my way to FAB and guiding brilliant young designers like the two of you," Mr. Kaye added. "So do not embarrass me."

Mickey and JC looked at each other. Mr. Kaye meant it. He left them waiting in the lobby and went to register.

"He sure knows how to turn a warm and fuzzy moment into a threat, doesn't he?" JC joked.

When their teacher returned, he was holding a single manila envelope. "Your ultimate challenge," he said. "It's assigned at random, so no team has any advantage. You get what you get, and you don't get upset."

He handed her the envelope, and she stood there staring at it. Then she closed her eyes and made a silent wish that it would be something good.

"If you're not opening it, I will," JC said anxiously.

Finally, Mickey tore open the envelope and read the paper inside several times.

"What does it say?" JC asked. "Spill it!"

"It says 'Fashion Hero,'" Mickey replied, puzzled. "That's it. Just two words."

"What does that even mean?" JC asked.

"It's entirely up to your interpretation," Mr. Kaye said. "A very FIFI assignment, as I anticipated. I suggest you two go sit in the FIFI yard and figure out what you want to make." He glanced at his watch. "The fabric stores open in an hour, and you have one hundred dollars to spend."

Mickey's eyes lit up. "One hundred dollars? Wow! We can really make something amazing with that much money."

JC dragged her to the front door. "Come on, come on. Time's a-tickin'!"

They found a quiet bench and began to brainstorm.

"I'm seeing a superhero design—maybe a cape, a mask. Ooh! Red spandex leggings?" Mickey said. She pulled out her sketchbook and a red colored pencil.

JC made a face. "Ew, that's cheesy. I think we should do a Madonna early-eighties ensemble."

"Madonna?" Mickey exclaimed. "Where do you get Madonna from?"

"Well, if there's one true fashion hero on this planet, it's her," JC said. "Can't you just see it: black lace leggings and combat boots! A tulle skirt and a leather bustier!"

Now it was Mickey's turn to make a face. "That's just so retro. I hate it."

"Well, I hate your idea," JC snapped back. "So we're even."

They continued arguing for another thirty

minutes. "What about a spiderweb skirt—ooh! With a batwing blouse!"

JC groaned. "What is she supposed to be? A confused superhero?"

"I suppose you have a better idea?" Mickey asked.

"Totally! Let's do a meat dress à la Lady Gaga— with a red lace hat over her eyes. Wait! We're in Paris, so let's make it an escargot dress!"

"Stop!" Mickey said, shaking her head. "No pop star, no snails."

"Fine—no more Spider-Man and Batman looks," JC shot back. "Next thing you know, you're going to make our model look like the Incredible Hulk."

Mickey held up a green colored pencil. "Now you're talkin'!"

JC grabbed the pencil out of her hand. "No way. Don't even think about it!"

Mr. Kaye came outside to find them.

"So, what have you come up with?" he asked.

"Nothing," JC huffed. "She doesn't like any of my ideas."

"And he thinks my ideas are cheesy!"

Mr. Kaye looked confounded. "Are you telling me you can't agree on a single design?"

Mickey and JC shook their heads in unison. "Nuh-uh."

"Well," their teacher said, "this is a less-than-ideal situation."

"Are you kidding?" JC shouted. "It's a disaster. Mickey wants to walk Supergirl down the runway!"

"I said Style Girl, not Supergirl," she interrupted.

"Same thing," JC insisted. "With a big gold *S* on her shirt. It's just too tacky. I can't. I really can't."

"Then don't!" Mickey suddenly shouted. "I don't need your help if that's how you feel. I'll make it myself."

"Fine!" JC fired back.

"Fine!" Mickey said.

"This is not fine—not by any means," Mr.

Kaye said, rubbing his temples. "You're supposed to be a team, and a team works together. If Mickey does this alone…"

"I'll win," she jumped in. "It's a great idea, Mr. Kaye, and I believe in it."

Mr. Kaye raised an eyebrow. "All right then, if you feel that strongly."

JC was fuming. He hadn't come all the way to Paris *not* to work on a design for the competition. He was one half of the team. But Mickey was being so stubborn…

"My cousin Angelique and I will enjoy a lovely day shopping while you slave over your design," he said. "Have a good time."

Mickey saw that he was hurt, but what choice did she have? There was no way she was going to send a Madonna costume down the runway. And JC just wouldn't give in. Sometimes he could be so bossy!

"I *will* have a great time—without you," she said. The words hung between them in the air, and she knew she didn't really mean them. But it was too late to take them back.

13

Amis pour le Vie

Mickey was still furious at JC when she and her mom left to find the fabric store Mr. Kaye had suggested. It was down a long street marked "Rue des Petits-Champs."

"It's so confusing," Mickey said, trying to read a city map. "All these streets sound alike—or should I say all these *rues*? It's all *rue* this' and *rue* that.'"

Her mom chuckled. "Well. I'm sure tourists

get very lost in New York City wandering around the Fashion District and Times Square," she said. "It's just as confusing for them."

"I think it's down there." Mickey pointed to a large, white building with a huge sign that read "Maison Tissu."

"It's either fabric—or a store dedicated to Kleenex!" her mom joked. They walked in the shop, and Mickey's jaw dropped. She had never seen so many bolts of fabric! The store was nearly a block long and three stories high.

"This place makes Plush look small," Mickey said. "How am I supposed to find anything?" She studied all the signs on the walls indicating the departments. "What do you suppose *laine fine* is?" she asked her mom.

"Beats me," her mother replied. "I thought JC was coming along to help."

Mickey sighed. If JC was here, he would have known where to find the red satin she needed. He would have had a ton of ideas too—like what gold braiding to use on the shoulders of the cape and what wool crepe would work best for the royal-blue skirt. "JC and I…we kinda decided to go our separate ways on this design."

Her mom looked concerned. "What? You and JC are a great team. What happened?"

Mickey shrugged and kept browsing the

aisles. "Nothing. We just couldn't see eye to eye."

"So that's it? Adios to your best friend at FAB because you don't agree?"

"It's 'au revoir' in French," Mickey corrected her. "And I didn't say good-bye—he did."

"How many times have we not agreed, Mickey? It's not a reason to give up on a relationship."

Mickey knew her mother was right, but JC had made it sound so final: "I'm outta here!" She could almost hear him saying it.

"*Où est le cachemire?*" said a voice. Funny, Mickey thought, it sounded just like JC! "I need something pink and pretty—*pour mon chien, Madonna.*"

Mickey spun around—it was JC!

"You!" she exclaimed.

"*Moi*," JC replied. "Guess Mr. Kaye sent us to the same fabric store."

"Well, I don't need your help," Mickey said.

"I wasn't offering it," JC replied. "I was just here with my cousin shopping for some new fabric for Madonna's Paris wardrobe."

"Oh," Mickey said. She'd secretly hoped he was there for her.

"Unless," JC said, "you need my help?"

Mickey's mom smiled. "Why don't I leave you two to talk."

Mickey stared down at her pink patent combat

boots. "Maybe the escargot dress wasn't all that awful," she began.

"Awful? It's genius," JC replied.

"I wouldn't say that..." Mickey piped up. "But it wasn't as bad as I made it sound. Maybe I should have been a little more open to your ideas and not just shot them down. JC, I'm—"

"Sorry," he interrupted. "I'm the one who's really sorry, Mick. I shouldn't have called your idea tacky. At least not till I saw it..."

"Hey," Mickey said, laughing. "It won't be tacky—I promise. Not if we work on it together." She took a deep breath. "Will you? Because I can't win this competition without you."

"Of course you can't," JC teased. "*Je suis fabuleuse!*"

Mickey scratched her head. "I'm not sure what you just said, but if it means you're the best, than I agree. Teammates?" She held out her hand for JC to shake.

"Teammates!" he replied, taking it. "And more importantly, *amis pour la vie*—friends forever."

14

★ A Scratchy Situation ★

With JC by her side, Mickey finished the fourth and final design for her collection in just a few days. The FIFI design studios were huge and had everything a designer could want: hundreds of threads, needles, and top-of-the-line sewing machines.

"The train on the cape makes all the difference," Mickey told him.

"Told ya so," JC said, making some quick adjustments on the hem. "It'll be such a wow moment."

The FIFI gala was just a few hours away, and backstage was bustling with activity. Designers were doing last-minute fittings; models were getting changed and having their hair and makeup done; and photographers were snapping it all.

"How is our FAB team doing?" Mr. Kaye asked, finding them in the crowd of students.

"Great—and right on schedule," Mickey answered, checking a list on her clipboard. "My mom is doing the models' makeup, and JC is on accessory patrol."

JC held up a black leather bootie. "Does this say superhero—or style zero?" he asked her.

She gave him the thumbs-up and continued,

"I really think we have it all under control, Mr. Kaye. I'm not nervous at all."

But she spoke too soon. Jade strutted in, and Jake followed close behind her, dragging several racks of garments. She had roped off a portion of the backstage area—the biggest and brightest space—and was now setting up shop.

"Did you call to see if Gisele was free?" Jade asked her brother. "I want only supermodels wearing my looks on the runway tonight."

Jake shook his head. "Negative. She's busy. But I got a maybe from Cara Delevingne."

"A maybe?" Jade gasped. "No one gives me a maybe. Does she *know* who I am?"

Jake pulled out his cell phone and started texting. "On it."

"They don't even have their models yet?" JC whispered to Mickey. "Can you say 'train wreck'?"

Mickey had no doubt that Jade would drum up some high-profile models in time for the show. But she did kind of enjoy watching her rival stress and squirm in the process.

"Jake!" Jade bellowed. "Why is my Eiffel Tower dress not steamed yet? And where is the Superman suit?" Jake pulled a jumpsuit off the rack. Half of it looked like a conservative business suit; the other half like a superhero costume.

Mickey couldn't believe her eyes. "How is that even possible?" she asked Mr. Kaye. "I thought every team got a different challenge."

"That is true," Mr. Kaye said, putting on his glasses to get a better look at Jade's design. "I'm not sure what happened."

"Well, I'm gonna find out!" Mickey said, and marched over to where Jade was standing.

"You stole my design...again," she accused Jade. "First French architecture, now this."

"*Excusez-moi?*" Jade said, batting her eyelashes. "Why would I *ever* steal from you? I have way too much taste to go digging in the garbage bin."

"Superman. How did you get Superman?"

Mickey continued. "Our challenge theme was Fashion Hero—so why do you have the same one?"

Jade snickered. "I don't. Mine was Under Cover, and Jake came up with the split design between Clark Kent and Superman."

"I'm a huge comic book buff," Jake explained. "Superman is really Clark Kent undercover."

"Oh," Mickey said, slightly embarrassed by her outburst. "So you just interpreted it that way."

"Do you have a problem?" Jade taunted her. "Because if you do, I'm happy to call over the head judge right now." She waved to a gentleman across the room.

"No, it's fine, really," Mickey backpedaled.

The last thing she needed was to call attention to herself with the head judge.

But Jade was determined. "Oh, Monsieur Roget!" she shouted. "Over here, *s'il vous plait*!"

Mr. Kaye's ears perked up. "He's head judge?"

Tony's smile grew wide as he strolled over. "Why yes, Chester, I am. And I know how happy you must be to hear it."

"Elated," Mr. Kaye replied sarcastically. "And since I know you never play fair, I suppose we should just pack our bags and go home right now."

Mickey stepped between them. "Oh no, we're not!" she protested. "I worked really hard on my collection, and I'm proud of it."

"Yeah," JC piped up. "We're here to rock this runway." He turned to his teacher. "Right, Mr. Kaye?"

"Oh, all right," he relented. "We'll stay."

"*Très bien!*" Tony said. "I'm looking forward to seeing your entry in the competition. I'm sure any students of Chester Kaye's are serious contenders."

Mr. Kaye looked up. Had Tony just paid him a compliment? "You mean that?"

"I do," Tony replied. "You seem to think I hate you—but I don't. I admire you greatly."

Mr. Kaye blushed. "Admire me? Years ago you told the FIFI administration I wasn't qualified to teach here."

"I told them *I* would be a great teacher—not that you would be a bad one. I stuck up for myself—how do you say, 'Tooted my own horn'? I can't help it if they liked what they heard."

"Did you toot too?" Mickey asked Mr. Kaye.

"No," he replied, scratching his head. "I don't recall having a lot of confidence in myself back then."

"Your teacher—he was very quiet and shy," Tony added.

Mickey laughed. "Mr. Kaye? Quiet?"

"I know, it boggles the mind," Mr. Kaye said. "But it's true. I always thought everyone—especially Gaston—was better than me."

"And I was not—that is clear," Tony said. "I was just better at talking a good game."

"Ah," JC said, nodding. "A branding genius. I get that. I'm always telling Mickey she has to create some buzz around her designs."

"*Exactement*," Tony said. Then he turned to Mr. Kaye. "I am sorry we didn't remain friends. We were the best of friends, and I'm sad to have lost that."

"Yes, well…" Mr. Kaye stammered. "Apology accepted."

Tony drew him into a huge hug, and Mr. Kaye squirmed. "You will come and be a guest lecturer at FIFI this summer, no?"

"No...I mean yes!" Mr. Kaye said. "I would like that."

"And I would like us to bury the ax," Tony said.

"Hatchet. Bury the hatchet," Mr. Kaye corrected him.

"Yes, that too!"

Mickey smiled: not only had she and JC made up, but Mr. Kaye and Tony had rekindled their friendship as well. That left only one person to smooth things out with. Mickey gritted her teeth but did the right thing.

"Jade," Mickey said, "your Superman look is great, and I know you and Jake came up with it fair and square."

"You do?" Jade looked confused. No one had ever accused her of playing fair before!

"I do. And I think we both have very strong collections to represent our school here in Paris. So whichever team wins, it's a win for FAB."

Jade was speechless; all the well-wishing made her feel uncomfortable. And come to think of it…itchy. She suddenly couldn't stop scratching at her arm.

"What are you doing?" Jake whispered to her.

"I dunno—I'm really itchy," she replied. She rolled up her sleeve and saw that her arm was covered in tiny, red bumps.

"Those look like hives," Mr. Kaye said, concerned. "Are you allergic to something?"

Jade panicked. "I dunno! Maybe it was that French brie cheese I had for lunch? Or the foie gras for dinner?"

"Or polyester!" Jake suddenly shouted. "You insisted on buying that silk material to use on the Superman cape! Polyester is the only thing that makes you break out in a rash like this."

Tony examined the fabric closely. "*Oui*, this is polyester satin," he said.

"What? The saleswoman charged me a fortune!" Jade insisted. "She said it was the finest silk she had."

"Well, she *did* say it in French," Jake reminded her. "Kinda fast. I told you we should have used Google Translate."

"Now what do I do?" Jade shouted. "I've been sewing that fabric all night for the show! It's getting worse by the minute!" The angrier she got, the more the hives spread till they were creeping up her neck and spreading to her back and stomach.

"I will have someone go with you back to the hotel, and I will call a doctor," Tony insisted. "Jake will present your collection."

"I will?" Jake said. "By myself?"

"You will—and you will do a fine job," Mr.

Kaye said, taking Jake aside and patting him on the back. "Time to toot your own horn."

Jade was scratching wildly. "Fine. Go present the collection. Just don't mess it up."

Jake went to hug her, but she screamed, "Don't touch me! I'm so itchy!"

"Bye, Jade! Don't do anything rash," JC called as Tony escorted Jade out of the FIFI gala. "Get it? Rash?"

Mickey giggled. "I don't know about you, but I'm itchin' for this competition to get started!"

She and JC were cracking up when Mr. Kaye shot them a stern look. "I'm glad you find this situation humorous. FAB's reputation is on the line." He looked at Mickey, JC, and Jake. "And it rests in your hands."

15

In the Spotlight

As the black-tie guests flooded into the FIFI gala banquet hall, Tony took the microphone to welcome them. "Esteemed guests from around the world," he began. "Welcome to the annual FIFI International Student Runway Invitational. The designers who are presenting here tonight are the best and brightest. They all have that certain je ne sais quoi, and their individual schools have chosen them as representatives."

The crowd was dressed in tuxedos and shimmering evening gowns, and the entire room was decorated with French flags and towering flower arrangements. The judges sat at a long table at the end of the runway, and they were some of the biggest names in French fashion.

"Monsieur Louboutin"—Tony waved to him from the stage—"we are deeply honored."

Mickey loved the look she'd made for herself: a cropped black tuxedo jacket splattered with paint and a matching tulle skirt. For her mom, she'd created a dress reminiscent of Leslie Caron in the movie *An American in Paris*: a sleeveless top striped with rainbow ribbons and a billowing orange chiffon skirt. JC had dressed up as well, in a blue velvet jacket with "tails." Madonna was equally stylish in a rhinestone-studded collar and matching blue-velvet dog bag.

They all waited frantically backstage for the show to begin.

"There are so many people out there," Mickey said, peeking out the curtain. "So many stylish people!"

"They look like they eat Americans for lunch," JC remarked.

Madonna barked. "It's okay, Madonna," JC assured her. "Chihuahuas are Mexican."

Tony clinked his glass to get the audience's attention. "Silence, *s'il vous plait,*" he said, signaling them to settle down. "It's time to start the runway show!"

As techno music pulsed over the speakers, the first designers to present were a team of British students from the London School of Fashion. Their representation of Paris was based on its legendary singer, Édith Piaf. Each look was rose-colored, like her song "La Vie en Rose."

"Stunning," JC remarked. "The dye work on that gown is to die for."

Mickey nodded. "They *are* really good."

Next up was a pair of Japanese students from Mod Tokyo School of Art and Design.

"Whoa," Jake said, whistling through his teeth.

"They used vinyl to create skirts that look like French perfume bottles."

Mickey agreed: this collection was even more innovative than the one before it.

"Next, please welcome our competitors from the Fashion Academy of Brooklyn…" Tony introduced them.

Mickey gulped and grabbed JC's hand. "OMG, that's us!"

She gave her first model a quick push onto the stage just as her mom was putting the finishing touches on the girl's lip gloss.

"She looks great, honey," Mickey's mother assured her. "They all do."

JC and Mickey watched anxiously for the crowd's reaction. The shredded Gauguin earned oohs and aahs, but the superhero cape and her Seurat dress got only lukewarm applause. Mickey was shocked: she loved the royal-blue column gown she and JC had created and the billowing red, white, and blue satin cape that appeared to "fly" as the model strutted down the runway.

"I don't think they understood it," Mickey said. "Maybe the paintings were too out there—or the cape was too long? Maybe I should have done blue not green—or fewer dots on the dress?"

"Honey, you can't second-guess yourself," her mom reminded her. "If you don't win this time, it's okay. We got to go to Paris, didn't we? Best trip ever!"

Tony's voice boomed over the speakers. "And now, we have yet another entry from the States, an independent team sponsored by House of Lee Couture…"

Mickey turned to Jake. "You gotta wow 'em."

"Me?" Jake asked. "Why me?"

"Because you're from FAB, and we stick together."

"Break a heel," JC said, wishing him good luck. Jake looked terrified and lost without his twin sister.

"What's wrong?" Mickey asked him gently.

"I-I just don't know what to do without Jade," he said. "I mean, she always handles the runway shows. I'm just in the background, sewing and styling."

JC gave him a shove. "Then it's time to take your place in the spotlight," he said. "You're an awesome designer, Jake. You don't have to hide in Jade's shadow."

Jake thought about what JC was saying. He saw his three supermodels looking to him for instructions.

"Do we have our next student presentation?" Tony called over the loudspeaker.

"Okay, ladies." Jake huddled his models

together. "Shoulders back, heads high. This collection is about long, strong lines, so no slouching!"

The girls all obeyed and strutted out onto the runway looking fierce and fab. The last look was Jake's "split personality" Clark Kent and Superman suit. As the model did a spin at the end of the runway, there was thunderous applause.

"Do you hear that?" Mickey asked him. "They love it. They love you."

Jake beamed. "They kinda do, don't they?"

"And there's not a sign of Jade in sight," JC reminded him. "You did this on your own—and that last design was all yours."

"Come on out here, Jake Lee," Tony said over

the microphone. "Take a bow for that incredible last look. *Très à la mode de l'avant*—very fashion forward!"

Jake blushed. "I'm proud to be a FAB student and represent my school," he said, glancing at Mickey. "FAB folks stick together."

Once all the students were done presenting, the judges deliberated for nearly an hour while the guests ate a gourmet French dinner.

"Pass the beef bourguignon," JC said, helping himself to seconds at their assigned table.

"How can you eat?" Mickey said nervously. "I'm a wreck."

"Oh, me too," JC said, helping himself to a cream puff for dessert. "I always eat when I'm stressed."

When the waiters had cleared all the courses, it was time for the awards to commence. Tony took to the stage, waving an envelope in his hand.

"Monsieurs and madames," he said. "May I have your attention please? The judges have decided."

There was a long list of medals: best needlework; most impressive embellishment; best use of unconventional materials. The Tokyo team and their perfume bottles took that prize.

Nearly halfway through the awards, FAB had still won nothing.

Mr. Kaye drummed his fingers on the table. "Come on, come on…" he said through clenched teeth.

Tony cleared his throat. "And now, the award for most colorful design: Mickey Williams and JC Cumberland from Fashion Academy of Brooklyn!"

"That's us!" JC cheered, leaping out of his seat to go retrieve their prize.

Tony hung a gold medal around each of their necks and congratulated them.

"I think the judges made the right decision," he told Mickey. "This category is *très* you."

Mickey smiled and held the medal up in the air so both Mr. Kaye and her mom could see it.

They took their seats while a few more medals were handed out. An Italian school took home "most accomplished leather crafting" for a chocolate-brown suede bubble coat inspired by a chocolate soufflé, and a German group earned "best use of luxe fabric" for its gold lamé gown that looked like the Dôme des Invalides. Jake wasn't among the winners, and he was beginning to lose hope.

"It's okay, Jake," Mickey said, patting him on the back. "No biggie."

Tony cleared his throat: "Last but not least, we have *le prix ultime*—the ultimate prize. This is the top award of the competition, and it goes to the design the judges felt was the most innovative and avant-garde." Jake peered out at the judges, but their faces were completely blank. *Oh well*, he thought, *Jade was right…she's the designer in the family, not me.*

Tony held up a huge, gold trophy cup. "And the winner is…Jake Lee, Fashion Academy of Brooklyn!"

"Whoopie!" Mr. Kaye yelled, jumping out of his seat. "FAB wins! We win!"

Jake sat and stared, utterly speechless.

"What are you waiting for? Get up there! Go get that trophy!" JC said, shaking him.

Timidly, Jake made his way up to the stage, and Tony handed him the gold cup.

"Tell the audience, where did you find your inspiration for your design?" he asked, pointing the microphone in Jake's face.

"I-I…" Jake stuttered. "I guess sometimes I feel like Clark Kent, hiding in the shadows, when I want to be a fashion superhero."

"You should stop hiding," Tony said, shaking his hand. "You are very talented."

Jake held tight to his trophy and took his seat at the table.

"Feels good, doesn't it?" Mickey asked him.

"Yeah," Jake said. "It does. It feels great to get credit for a change."

Mr. Kaye was beside himself. All the judges

rushed up to shake his hand and congratulate him on his school's top placement in the invitational.

"*Bon travail!* Good job!" Christian Louboutin said, patting him on the back.

Mr. Kaye blushed. "*Merci, merci!*"

"I'm not surprised FAB won the top prize," Tony told the judges. "Chester is a brilliant teacher. I saw for myself when I visited New York City recently. He fights hard for his students."

Mr. Kaye shrugged. "Well, I-I try."

"You do more than try," Tony said. "You help these kids believe in themselves. You empower them."

Mr. Kaye held his head high. "I do, don't I? Let me tell you my educational philosophy…"

"Great," JC whispered to Mickey. "Now there'll be no talking to him."

Mickey giggled. It was great to see Mr. Kaye so happy. Come to think of it, she'd *never* actually seen him laugh before. This was a first!

"I'm proud of you, Mickey Mouse," her mom said, admiring Mickey's medal. "That's quite a prize you've got there."

The best part, Mickey thought, was that she had proved she belonged on the Paris runway—and she knew she'd be back again one day.

"I can't believe we're leaving tomorrow," she said. "The week flew by."

JC looked at his watch. "There's still time to hit my favorite patisserie."

Come to think of it, Mickey *was* starving. "Do you think they have macarons?" she asked.

"One Mickey macaron coming up!" JC said.

Carrie's Style File

**Meet Susanna Paliotta and Isabella Barrett,
designers of Bound by the Crown Couture for kids!**

Bound by the Crown Couture is a kids' couture
fashion label for trendy four- to fourteen-year-
olds. I went to their runway show during New
York Fashion Week and was wowed by how so-
phisticated and chic their line is—and how well
the mom-daughter duo work together! I love how
the clothes feel cool and classic at the same time,

from the tweed suits to the ornate "angel" gowns.
The look was very grown-up but also age appro-
priate. So how do they do it? I had to ask! Check
out boundbythecrown.com to see and shop some
of their latest looks!

**Carrie: My mom and I write our book series
together. How do you two work together as a
design team?**

Susanna: Bella is very involved in the fabric
choices. She loves going to the outlets and seeing
all the samples and has a very clear vision of what
kids like. It helps to have that perspective when
building a children line.

There is no better way to do test market research than when Bella wears something and we get to see what type of reaction people give before putting it into full production.

Carrie: What's the hardest part of working together?

Susanna: Separating the family aspect from business. Sometimes it's hard not to be Mom! But I respect Bella's opinion.

Carrie: How do you decide what looks will be "in" for the new season?

Susanna: Trend forecasting is one of the hardest

but most fun aspects of fashion design! The BBTC brand likes to stay with vintage styles while using modern fabrics, so even when we are trend forecasting, we are staying true to the brand's core values.

Carrie: How and why did you decide to create your own fashion line for kids?

Susanna: After buying hundreds of "one and done" outfits for Bella—most of which were uncomfortable—she said to me we should make "comfortable couture." I knew she was right; this is what kids want. I made a few samples based on styles I grew up wearing but let Bella choose the fabrics, and we got a huge positive response.

Carrie: Bella, you're a serious entrepreneur! What advice do you have for kids who want to start their own business?

Bella: I have grown up in a family that all owned their own businesses—so I knew I wanted to own my own as well. My advice is do something you love! When you're young, you can try different hobbies, and the best part of being a kid is there are no boundaries on your ideas! Through the Young Entrepreneur Club, I have met so many kids who started businesses in their playrooms. Don't be afraid to dream big.

Carrie: How would you describe "fashion"?

Bella: Fashion is a way to express yourself.

Susanna: It's the best form of expression! What I love most about fashion is you can have the same outfit and put it on three different girls, and they will all wear it a little different.

Here I am with Susanna modeling one of her chic BBTC coats. Love!

Acknowledgments

Many thanks to our families—the Kahns, the Berks, and the Saps—for their continued love and support!

To the gang at Vital Theatre (especially Steve, Sam, Annjolynn, Shani, Kyle, Julz, Holly, and Jamie) and all the brilliant actors (Kayla, Rachel, Alexis, Luke, Brie) who brought Mickey and company to life for the very first time! Love you guys and so appreciate all your hard work and dedication to the show. Sabrina: you were a blast to work with and a generous collaborator. We had tons of laughs, tears, and way too much coffee in the green room. Thank you for loving Fashion Academy and pouring your heart, soul, and music into it. Next stop, Fashion Academy: The Tour!!!! ;-) Jill Jaysen: you threw the biggest, best opening night bash EVER (Tinkerbelle!!!!). Thank you so much for your enthusiasm and above-and-beyond efforts. xo

To our Sourcebooks team: Steve, Kate, Elizabeth—we couldn't do it without you.

To Katherine Latshaw at Folio: we love that

you always come to opening night and are our biggest cheerleader!

To Ms. Sayers: thanks for teaching Carrie to sew on a machine for the very first time! She will always treasure her tote bag and apron she made in your mini-term class and has a newfound appreciation for perfectly straight stitches!

DON'T MISS MICKEY'S NEXT

FABULOUS FASHION ADVENTURE!

Model Madness

About the Authors

Sheryl Berk has written about fashion for more than twenty years, first as a contributor to *InStyle* magazine and later as the founding editor in chief of *Life & Style Weekly*. She has written dozens of books with celebrities including Britney Spears, Jenna Ushkowitz, Whitney Port, and Zendaya—and the #1 *New York Times* bestseller (turned movie) *Soul Surfer*

with Bethany Hamilton. Her daughter, Carrie Berk, is a renowned cupcake connoisseur and blogger (www.facebook.com/PLCCupcakeClub; https://carriescupcakecritique.shutterfly.com) with more than 100,000 followers at the age of thirteen! Carrie is a fountain of fabulous ideas for book series—she came up with Fashion Academy in the fifth grade. Carrie learned to sew from her grandma "Gaga" and has outfitted many an American Girl doll in original fashions. The Berks also write the deliciously popular series The Cupcake Club.

Check out Carrie's new fashion blog: fashionacademybook.com and Instagram: @fashionacademybook.